# READY, ALICE?

READY, ALICE?

*Simultaneously published in hardcover with library binding
and trade paper / June 1990
"Bantam Little Rooster" is a trademark of Bantam Books.*

**Library of Congress Cataloging-in-Publication Data**
Mason, Margo.
  Ready, Alice? / written by Margo Mason, illustrated by Catherine
Siracusa.
      p.  cm.
  "A Bantam little rooster book."
  Summary: Alice takes her time getting up, getting dressed, eating
breakfast; and getting ready for the beach.
  ISBN 0-553-05816-9.—ISBN 0-553-34741-1 (pbk.)
  [1. Behavior—Fiction.]  I. Siracusa, Catherine, ill.  II. Title.
PZ7.M414Re  1989
[E]—dc19                                               88-37366
                                                            CIP
                                                            AC

Published simultaneously in the United States and Canada

PRINTED IN THE UNITED STATES OF AMERICA

0  9  8  7  6  5  4  3  2  1

JER

# READY, ALICE?

by Margo Mason
Pictures by Catherine Siracusa

A BANTAM LITTLE ROOSTER BOOK
NEW YORK · TORONTO · LONDON · SYDNEY · AUCKLAND

"Time to get up, Alice."

"Not yet," said Alice.

But it looked like a nice day.
So Alice got out of bed.

"Time to get dressed, Alice."

"Not yet," said Alice.

# But Alice got dressed.

She put on her shirt…

her jeans…

her socks…

and her shoes.

"Time for breakfast, Alice."

"Not yet," said Alice.

But it looked like a nice day.

So Alice went downstairs.

"Good morning, Alice,"
said her mother.

"Good morning, Alice,"
said her father.

"Ready for breakfast, Alice?"

"Not yet," said Alice.

But Alice drank her juice
and took six bites of toast.

"Don't want my egg, Mom,"
said Alice.

"Eat it up," said Mom.
"You'll be hungry later."

Alice hit the top of the egg
with her fork.

"Careful, Alice!" said her mother

"What a mess!" said her father.

Alice went upstairs.

She went to the bathroom
to wash.

"Are you ready, Alice?"
called her mother.

"Not yet," said Alice.

"Well, we're waiting,"
said Dad. "Would you like
to go to the beach today?"

Alice went to her room.
She took off her shoes
and put on her sandals.

She took off her jeans
and put on her shorts.

Alice found her sunhat…

her pail and shovel…

her boat…

her water pistol…

and her net.

"You must be ready now!"
shouted her father.

Alice put on her sunhat.

"Ready!" said Alice.